Austin from Boston

Jacqueline Matte

FATCAT
PUBLISHING

Shawn Brasfield

Library of Congress Catalog Card Number 97-60783
Matte, Jacqueline
Austin from Boston/by Jacqueline Matte; illustrated by Shawn Brasfield
p. cm.

First Edition 10 9 8 7 6 5 4 3 2 1
ISBN 0-9654721-0-8

Published by Fat Cat Publishing
A subsidiary of Max Productions, Inc.
8601 Dunwoody Place, Suite 502
Atlanta, Georgia 30350

The illustrations in this book were created using watercolor,
gouache, pen-n-ink, and various other colorful mediums.
The display type was handlettered by Shawn Brasfield.
The text type was set in Avenir.
Color separations by Bright Arts, Hong Kong
Printed in Hong Kong and bound in China by Imago
Designed by Brasfield Illustration Co.

*A portion of the proceeds from the sale of each book
is donated to Shepherd Center in Atlanta, Georgia.
Shepherd Center is a private, not-for-profit hospital specializing
in the care of people with spinal cord injury and disease,
acquired brain injury, multiple sclerosis and other neuromuscular diseases
and urological disorders.*

This book is dedicated
with love and affection to my grandchildren,
Austin, Katie and Sean.

Once upon a time ago,

in a place called

Boston

lived a friendly little boy
by the name of

Austin

Of course he had a Mom and Dad,
but no one else at all,
whom he could run and play with,
or even catch a ball.

When Austin turned just 5 years old,
his folks surprised the lad,
with the GREATEST present that
a boy could ever have.

A dog with soft and floppy ears,
his tail was wagging too
and Austin called this little dog,
his SILLY MACADOO!

They spent a lot of happy times,
that little boy and pup
learning tricks and having fun
as they were growing up.

While in another part of town,
there was a little lady.
She lived in a mansion and
her parents called her Katie!

And Katie had a *different* pet
from all the pets she knew,
with strong hind legs and secret pouch,
it was a KANGAROO!

She named her strange pet Joey,
because her Dad had said,
baby 'roos were called just that,
at least that's what he'd read.

Over on Delancy Street,
where houses had no lawn,
lived one other little kid
whose name was simply Sean.

A parrot was his *only* pet,
'twas white with eyes of blue,
a right smart bird
who learned to speak,
it was a COCKATOO!

She was a fussy Polly and
she didn't like it much,
when people tried to handle her,
her feathers they would touch!

Now a guy named Wicked William –
A LIAR AND A FAKE,
would sometimes go into a house
to see what he could take.

And one day when the kids were out
and no one was at home,
William stole poor Macadoo —
he *even* took his bone!

He also took the kangaroo
and put him in the van,
and grabbed the fussy Polly too,
OH WHAT A WICKED MAN!

So Macadoo was stolen
and Austin's heart was sad,
Joey too was taken,
and Katie cried real bad.

And Sean up on Delancy Street,
was quite beside himself,
when he discovered Polly,
was missing from her shelf!

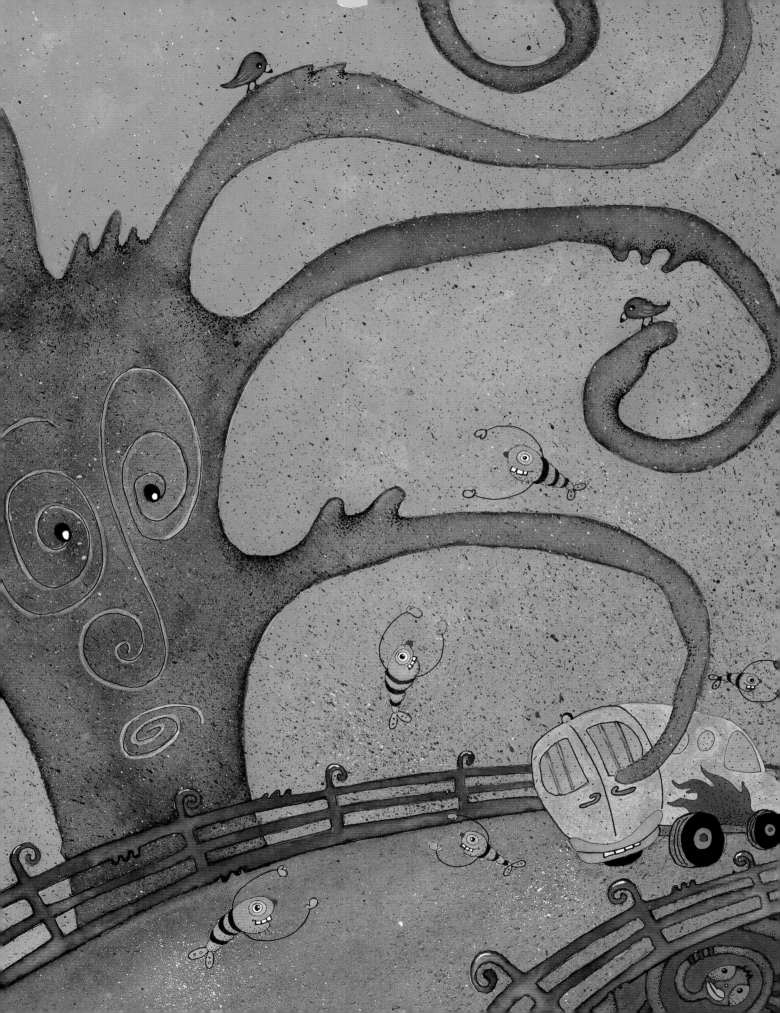

Each year when springtime came around
and summer days were near,
a carnival would come to town
and *suddenly* appear...

To raise its high and pointed tent
and set up all its rides,
inviting children and their folks
to pay and come inside.

And when the show arrived in town,
Will took those stolen pets,
to see if he could sell them
and see how much he'd get.

The bossman of the carnival,
could not believe his eyes,
when Joey jumped and Polly spoke,
HE REALLY WAS SURPRISED!

And when he saw how Macadoo
performed his many tricks,
the bossman paid off Wicked Will
and got him out real quick!

Because the pets were *always* good
and did as they were told,
the bossman was quite nice to them
and treated them like gold.

Joey jumped through flaming hoops,
while Polly from her swing,
talked to all the boys and girls
– she even had to sing!

And Silly Macadoo became
the center of attention,
when people saw the tricks he knew
– too many here to mention!

But these special animals
were often sad and blue,
because they missed their owners,
especially Macadoo.

He thought of little Austin,
who loved him from the start,
who'd let him curl up in his bed,
IT *REALLY* BROKE HIS HEART!

The carnival kept traveling,
the days and weeks just flew,
until, before you knew it,
another year was through.

Once again the show came to
that city known as Boston,
and in the audience this time,
there was a boy named Austin.

Sean was there and Katie too,
to see the famous show,
it was their first time ever,
and how were they to know...

That cockatoo and kangaroo
and Macadoo would be...
the very *first* attractions that
the crowd was going to see!

So excited were those kids,
when their pets they saw,
they screamed and shouted
out their names,
IT WAS A MIGHTY ROAR!

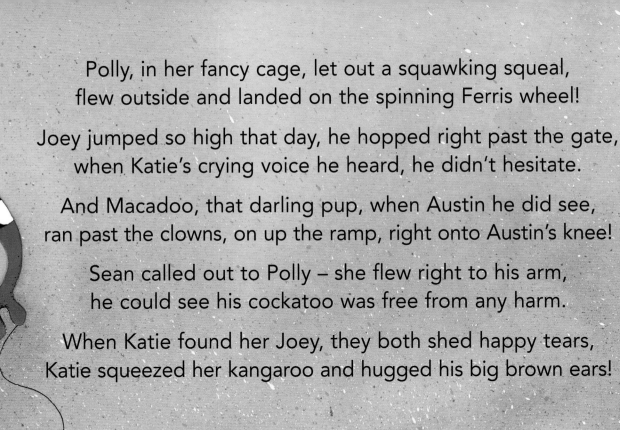

Polly, in her fancy cage, let out a squawking squeal,
flew outside and landed on the spinning Ferris wheel!

Joey jumped so high that day, he hopped right past the gate,
when Katie's crying voice he heard, he didn't hesitate.

And Macadoo, that darling pup, when Austin he did see,
ran past the clowns, on up the ramp, right onto Austin's knee!

Sean called out to Polly – she flew right to his arm,
he could see his cockatoo was free from any harm.

When Katie found her Joey, they both shed happy tears,
Katie squeezed her kangaroo and hugged his big brown ears!

As for little Austin, well,
there's not that much more to say,
except that one small boy's BIG smile,
lit up the sky that day!

And though the bossman felt quite sad,
to see the pets depart,
he knew that it was for the best –
he knew it in his heart.

'Cause pets belong with boys and girls,
who share their fun and laughter,
to love a pet means keeping it,
forever, ever after!!!